Théophile Gautier, Susan Coolidge

My Household of Pets

Théophile Gautier, Susan Coolidge

My Household of Pets

ISBN/EAN: 9783337396015

Printed in Europe, USA, Canada, Australia, Japan

Cover: Foto ©Andreas Hilbeck / pixelio.de

More available books at **www.hansebooks.com**

Théophile Gautier.

MY

Household of Pets.

Translated

By SUSAN COOLIDGE.

WITH ILLUSTRATIONS.

BOSTON:
ROBERTS BROTHERS.
1882.

CONTENTS.

ILLUSTRATIONS.

———•———

MY HOUSEHOLD OF PETS.

CHAPTER I.

OLD TIMES.

CARICATURES are in existence which represent us clothed in Turkish fashion, sitting cross-legged on cushions, and surrounded by cats, who are fearlessly climbing over our shoulders and even upon our head. Caricature is nothing more than the exaggeration of truth; and truth compels us to own that for animals in general, and for cats in particular, we have, all our lives long, had the tenderness of a Brahmin or of an old maid. The illustrious Byron carried a menagerie of pets about with him even

when on his travels, and raised a tomb
at Newstead Abbey to his faithful Newfoundland, " Boatswain," which bears an
epitaph of the poet's own composition.
But although we thus share his tastes,
we must not be accused of plagiarism;
for in our case the tendency manifested
itself even before we had begun to learn
the alphabet.

We are told that a clever man is about
to prepare a " History of Educated Animals;" so we offer him these notes, from
which, so far as our animals are concerned, he will be able to extract reliable
information.

Our earliest recollections of this nature
date back to our arrival in Paris from
Tarbes. We were then precisely three
years of age, — a fact which renders difficult of belief the statements of MM. de
Mirecourt and Vapereau, who assert, that
at that time we had already " received a

bad education" in our native city. A homesickness of which one would hardly believe so young a child to be capable took possession of us. We could speak only in *patois*, and those who expressed themselves in French seemed to us like foreigners and aliens. In the middle of the night we would wake up and disconsolately ask if we might not soon be allowed to go back to our own country.

No dainty could tempt us to eat. No plaything gave amusement. Drums and trumpets even, failed to rouse us from our melancholy. Among the things most mourned over was a dog named Cagnotte who had necessarily been left behind. His absence produced such wretchedness that, one morning, after having thrown out of window our tin soldiers, a German village painted in gaudy colors, and our reddest of red fiddles, we were on the point of following by the same road in

hopes of finding the sooner Tarbes, Gas-
cony and Cagnotte, and were only dragged
back in the very nick of time by the collar
of our jacket. The happy thought occurred to Josephine, our nurse, to tell us
that Cagnotte, impatient at being separated from us, was coming to Paris that
very day in the diligence. Children accept the incredible with an artless faith;
nothing seems impossible to their minds;
but it is dangerous to deceive them, for
once their opinions are formed the attempt to alter them is hopeless. All that
day long we asked every quarter of an
hour if Cagnotte had not come yet. At
last, to pacify us, Josephine went out and
bought on the *Pont Neuf* a little dog who
somewhat resembled the dog of Tarbes.
At first we were mistrustful, and would
not believe him to be the same; but we
were assured that travelling produces
strange changes in the looks of dogs.

This explanation was satisfactory, and the dog of the Pont Neuf was received as the authentic Cagnotte. He was an amiable dog, gentle and pretty. He licked our cheeks amicably, and his tongue condescended to stretch farther and extend itself to the bread-and-butter which had been cut for our luncheon. The best understanding existed between us. In spite of this, the false Cagnotte little by little became sad, dull, and constrained in his motions. He no longer curled himself up easily for a nap; all his joyous agility vanished; he panted for breath, and ate nothing. One day, when caressing him, we discovered on his stomach what appeared to be a seam, tightly stretched as if swollen. The nurse was called; she came, she cut a thread with the scissors, and lo! Cagnotte, emerging from a sort of jacket of curly lamb's-wool with which the dealers on the Pont Neuf had invested him in order that he might pass for a poodle, stood revealed in all his poverty and ugliness as a common street cur, ill-bred and valueless. He had grown fat, and his tight garments were suffocating him. Relieved from his cuirass, he shook his ears, stretched his legs, and gambolled joyfully round the room, not at all disquieted at his own ugliness, now that he once more found himself at ease. His appetite came back, and in his moral qualities we found compensation for his loss of good looks. In the companionship of Cagnotte, who was a true child of Paris, we forgot by slow degrees Tarbes and the high mountains which we had been used to see from our windows. We learned French, and we also became Parisian.

Let no one suppose that this is an imaginary tale invented to amuse the reader. The facts are strictly true, and they show that the dog-merchants of that period were

as ingenious as are the jockeys of to-day
in disguising their wares to cheat unsus-
pecting country-folk.

After the death of Cagnotte our affec-
tions turned to cats as more truly domestic
animals and better friends for the fireside.
We will not attempt to give a detailed history of all of them. Whole dynasties of
felines, as numerous as those of the Egyptian kings, succeeded one another in our
house; accident, death, escape, in turn
carrying them away. All were loved, and
all were regretted; but life is made up of
forgettings, and the remembrance of de-
parted cats is gradually effaced like the
remembrance of men.

It is a sad fact that the lives of these
humble friends, our inferior brothers, are
not better proportioned to those of their
masters.

After briefly alluding to an old gray cat,
who took our part against our own flesh

and blood, and bit our mother's ankles whenever she scolded or seemed about to punish us, we pass on to Childebrand, a cat belonging to the days of romance. From his name the reader will detect the secret desire which we felt to dispute Boileau, whom at that time we did not love, though since we have made peace with him. Does he not make Nicolas say :—

" Oh charming thought of poet, most ignorant and bland,
Among so many heroes to choose out Childebrand " ?

It did not seem to us that it argued such a depth of ignorance to select a hero of whom no one knew anything. Beside Childebrand struck us as an impressive name ; very long-haired, very Merovingian, Gothic and Mediæval to the last degree, and much to be preferred to a Grecian name,—be it Agamemnon, Achilles, Idomeneus, Ulysses, or any other. These names, however, were the fashion of the day, especially among young people ; for — to use a phrase taken from the notice of Kaulbach's frescoes on the outside of the Pinacothek at Munich — "Never did the Hydra of wigginess dress more bristling heads than at that period ; " and persons of a classical turn doubtless gave their cats such names as Hector, Ajax, or Patrocles. Our Childebrand was a magnificent cat of the house-tops, with shaven hair, striped fawn-color and black like Saltabadil's clown in " Le Roi s'Amuse." His great green eyes of almond shape, and his velvet, striped coat, gave him a resemblance to a tiger, which we found extremely pleasing ; for, as we have elsewhere said, cats are nothing more than tigers under a cloud. Childebrand has the honor to figure in some verses of ours, also intended for the discomfiture of Boileau : —

Then I for you will paint that picture of Rembrandt
Which pleases me most greatly; and meanwhile Childe-
 brand,
According to his custom soft couched upon my knee,
Lifts up his pretty head and watches anxiously
The movement of my finger, which traces in the air
The outline of the picture to make it clear and fair.

Childebrand came in nicely as a rhyme to Rembrandt; for this fragment was a sort of confession of faith and romance to a friend, since dead, who at that time shared all our enthusiasms for Victor Hugo, Sainte-Beuve, and Alfred de Musset.

We must say of our cats as said Ruy Gomez de Silva to the impatient Don Carlos, when giving him the names and titles of his ancestors, which began with "Don Silvius, three times elected Consul of Rome," "I have skipped some of the best——," and so pass on to Madame Theophile, a reddish cat, with a white breast, pink nose, and blue eyes, who was thus named because she lived with us in an almost conjugal intimacy, sleeping on the foot of our bed, or on the arm of our writing chair; following us in our walks in the garden, assisting at our meals, and not infrequently intercepting the morsels which we were conveying from our plate to our mouth.

One day a friend, who was leaving home for a short time, left in our charge a favorite parrot. The bird, feeling lonely in a strange house, climbed by the help of his beak to the top of the perch, and sat there rolling about in a scared way his eyes, which glittered like gilt nails, and wrinkling over them the white membranes which served for eyelids. Madame Theophile had never before encountered a parrot, and the novelty awoke in her mind an evident astonishment. Motionless as an Egyptian cat embalmed in its network of bandages, she sat regarding the bird with an air of profound meditation, and putting together

all the ideas of natural history which she
had been able to collect during her excursions on the roofs or in the courtyard and
garden. The shadows of her thoughts
flitted across her changeful eyes, and it
was not difficult to read the decision at
which she finally arrived: " This is — de-
cidedly it is — a green chicken ! "

This conclusion reached, the cat jumped
from the table which she had chosen as
her observatory, and crouched in a corner
of the room, her belly on the floor, her
knees bent, her head lowered, her spine
stiffened like that of the black panther
in Gérome's picture as it glares at the
gazelles who are drinking by the lake.

The parrot followed each movement of
the cat with a feverish disquietude. His
feathers bristled; he rattled his chain,
raised one of his claws and exercised its
talons, while he whetted his beak on the
edge of the feeding cup. Instinct revealed

AS FOR THE EYES OF THE CAT THEY WERE RIVETED
ON THE BIRD WITH A FASCINATED INTENSITY.

to him that this was an enemy who was plotting mischief.

As for the eyes of the cat, they were riveted on the bird with a fascinated intensity, and said plainly as eyes could speak, and in a language which the parrot understood only too well, "Green though he be, this chicken is without doubt good to eat."

While we watched this scene with interest, ready to interfere whenever it should seem necessary, Madame Theophile was imperceptibly drawing nearer to her prey. Her pink nose quivered, her eyes were half shut, her elastic claws projected and then disappeared again in their velvet sheaths. Little shivers ran down her spine: she was like an epicure as he seats himself at table before a dish of truffled chicken, and smacks his lips in advance over the choice and succulent repast which he is about to enjoy. This exotic dainty tickled all her sensuous capabilities.

Suddenly her back curved like a bow which is bent, and with one strong elastic bound she alighted on the perch. The parrot, seeing his danger, remarked in a deep bass voice, as low and solemn as that of M. Joseph Prudhomme, "Hast thou breakfasted, Jacquot?"

This remark created in the mind of the cat an evident dismay. She took a sudden leap backward. A blast from a trumpet, a pile of plates crashing to the floor, a pistol shot close to the ear, could not have inspired more sudden and giddy terror in an animal of her race. All her ornithological ideas were in one fell moment overturned.

"And on what? On the roast beef of the king?" continued the parrot.

The face of the cat now said, as distinctly as words, "This is not a bird. It is a gentleman! He speaks!"

"When I on wine have feasted free,
The tavern turns around with me,"

sang the bird in a tremendous voice; for
he perceived that the alarm caused by his
words was his readiest means of defence.
The cat cast a questioning glance toward
us, and, getting no reassurance in reply,
took refuge under the bed, from which
place of safety she could not be enticed for
the remainder of that day.

People who are not accustomed to live
with animals, or who, like Descartes, see
nothing in them but irrational organisms,
will no doubt suppose that these designs
and reflections which we attribute to birds
and beasts, are pure inventions of our
fancy. In this they are mistaken: we
but interpret their ideas, and faithfully
translate them into human speech.

Next day Madame Theophile, regaining
courage, made another attempt on the parrot, which was repulsed in the same way.

After that she gave it up, and accepted the
bird as a man.

This sensitive and charming animal
adored perfumes. Patchouli, the scent of
cashmeres, threw her into ecstasies. She
had also a taste for music; perched upon
a pile of score, she would listen attentively
and with evident pleasure to vocalists who
came to test their voices at our piano and
receive criticism. Sharp notes, however,
made her nervous, and at the upper "la"
she was apt to close the mouth of the
songstress with a tap of her little paw. It
was an experiment which caused us much
amusement, and was unfailing. Our feline
amateur never mistook the note, and never
let it pass unrebuked.

THE WHITE DYNASTY.

CHAPTER II.

THE WHITE DYNASTY.

L ET us now come down to a more
modern epoch. From a cat im-
ported by Mademoiselle Aita de la Pen-
uela, a young Spanish artist whose studies
of white Angoras adorned and still adorn
the windows of the print-shops, we obtained
the tiniest possible kitten, which looked
like one of those puffs of swan's-down
which people use in rice-powder boxes.
On account of this immaculate whiteness,
he received the name of Pierrot, which, as
he grew larger, was amplified into that of
Don Pierrot de Navarre, — a name infi-
nitely more majestic and having a savor of
real grandeur about it. Don Pierrot, like

all animals who are petted and spoiled grew up charmingly amiable. He shared our family life with that enjoyment which cats find in being admitted to the intimacies of the fire-side. Seated in his wonted place beside the fire, he seemed always to understand the conversation and to be interested in it. He followed the eyes of the talkers, emitting from time to time a little mew, as if he too had objections to make, and would like to add his opinion on the literary topics which were usually the theme of our discourse. He adored books; and whenever he found one lying open on the table he would seat himself by it, looking earnestly at the pages, and sometimes gently turning one with his claw. He usually finished by going to sleep, as soundly as though he had in reality been reading a modern novel!

When we sat down to write he always jumped upon the writing-table, and watched

with a profound attention the point of the
steel pen as it scattered flies' legs over the
white surface of the paper, making a little
movement of his head at the beginning of
each new line. Sometimes he took a fancy
to join in the work, and would try to get
the pen away from us, doubtless with the
intention of using it in his turn; for he
was an æsthetic cat, like the cat Murr, described by Hoffman, and we strongly sus-
pected him of spending nights in some
hidden gutter writing his memoirs by the
light of his own phosphoric eyes. Unfor-
tunately these lucubrations, if they ever
existed, are forever lost.

Don Pierrot de Navarre would never set-
tle himself to sleep till we had come home.
He always waited just inside the door,
and, the moment we stepped into the antechamber, rubbed himself against our legs,
arching his back, and purring in a joyous
and friendly manner. Then he would

walk in, preceding us like a page, and no
doubt with a very little urging would
have consented to carry the candlestick.

Having thus conducted us to our bed-
room, he waited till we were undressed, and
then, jumping into bed, embraced our neck
with his little paws, rubbed his nose against
ours, and licked us with a small pink
tongue, rough as a file, uttering meanwhile
short, inarticulate cries, which expressed as
clearly as possible his joy at our return.
Then, having expressed his affection by
these demonstrations, and the hour for
sleep being come, he would mount the
head-board of the bed, and slumber there,
poised like a bird on a bough. As soon
as we awoke in the morning he would descend, and, stretching himself out close to
us, wait quietly till it was time to get up.

Midnight, in his opinion, was the hour
at which it was our duty to return to the
house. Pierrot and the *concierge* were

PIERROT.

entirely of one mind on this point. Just
then we had joined with a few friends in
getting up a little club, which we called
" The Society of the Four Candles," from
the fact that the room in which we met
was lighted by four candles in silver can-
dlesticks, which were placed on four cor-
ners of a table. Sometimes the talk became
so engrossing that, like Cinderella, we forgot the hour, at the risk of finding our
carriages changed into pumpkins and our
coachmen into rats. Several times Pierrot waited for our return until two or
three o'clock in the morning; then his feel-
ings were so deeply hurt that he actually
went to bed without us. This dumb pro-
test against our innocent irregularities was
so touching that afterwards we made a
point of coming in punctually at midnight;
but Pierrot for a long while retained a
grudge against us. He wanted proof that
our penitence was genuine; and not till

time had convinced him of the sincerity of
our regret did he again take us into favor,
and resume his old position inside the door
of the antechamber.

A cat's friendship is a hard thing to
conquer. Cats are philosophical animals,
— sedate, quiet, fixed in their habits, true
believers in decency and order, and not at
all given to the bestowing of a thoughtless
affection. They will be your friends if
you prove worthy of friendship; but they
will never be your slaves. Even in mo-
ments of tenderness a cat preserves his
freedom of will, and cannot be made to
comply with demands which seem to him
unreasonable. But once he surrenders
himself to you as a friend, what absolute
confidence he gives! what fidelity of affection! He constitutes himself the companion of your solitary hours, of your
melancholy, of your work. He will pass
whole evenings purring on your knees,

happy in your company, and forsaking that of animals of his own species. In vain do enticing mews re-echo from the roofs, calling him to join one of those cat-soirees where juicy red-herrings take the place of tea: he will not be tempted away, and shares your vigil to the end. If you put him on the floor, he jumps back to his place with a murmuring noise which is like a soft reproach. Sometimes, standing near, he looks at you with eyes so full of melting tenderness, so loving and so human, that you are half-frightened; for it seems impossible that in such a regard reason can be lacking.

Don Pierrot de Navarre had a companion of the same race, no less white than himself. All the comparisons which we have heaped together in " The symphony in white, major " cannot express the idea of this immaculate snowiness, which makes even the fur of the ermine look yellow.

This second cat was named Seraphita, in
honor of Balzac's Swedenborgian romance.
Never did the heroine of that marvel-
lous legend radiate a purer whiteness, not
even when, accompanied by Minna, she
climbed the icy peaks of the Falberg.
Seraphita was of a contemplative and
dreamy disposition. She would lie for long
hours on her cushion, not asleep, but following, with an intense expression of the
eyes, sights which were invisible to common mortals. She liked to be caressed;
but she caressed in return only a favored
few to whom her hard-won esteem was
accorded. She loved luxury; and it was
always upon the softest chair and the piece
of stuff best calculated to show to advan-
tage her swan-like fur that we were sure to
find her. Her toilet took an enormous
deal of time; every particle of her fur was
made glossy each morning of her life. She
washed herself with her paws; and every

hair of her coat, carefully brushed with her rosy tongue, glistened like new silver. Whenever any one stroked her, she instantly removed all trace of the contact: the least untidiness disturbed her. Her elegance and distinction were truly aristocratic: in the cat-world she must have ranked as a duchess at the very least. She doted on perfumes, plunging her head into bouquets of flowers, and nibbling with little quivers of satisfaction handkerchiefs steeped in odors. She would walk up and down the dressing-table sniffing at the essence bottles, and would willingly have allowed herself to be dipped bodily into the scented rice-powder. Such was Seraphita, and never did a cat better justify a poetical name.

About this time two of those counterfeit sailors who sell striped table-covers, handkerchiefs woven of pineapple thread, and other foreign commodities, chanced to pass through our street at Longchamps. They carried in a tiny cage two Norway rats, with the prettiest pink eyes in the world. White animals were a passion with us just then, and we carried this passion so far that even our poultry-yard was stocked with white cocks and hens. We bought the white rats, and had a large cage made for them, with interior staircases which led to different stories, — to dining-rooms, sleeping-chambers, and gymnasiums fitted up with trapezes. In this cage they were happier and better lodged than even the rat of La Fontaine in the middle of his Dutch cheese.

These pretty creatures — of which so many people, for reasons that we cannot understand, have a silly fear — grew tame to an astonishing degree, so soon as they became certain that no harm was intended them. They allowed themselves to be stroked like kittens; and taking our finger between their tiny pink paws, delicate to an ideal degree, would lick it in a friendly way. They were usually let loose at the end of our meals, and climbing on our arms, shoulders, and head, would dart in and out of the sleeves of our jacket or dressing-gown with singular skill and agility. The motive of all these exercises, so gracefully performed, was to win leave to rummage among the remains of the dessert. Placed upon the table, in the twinkling of an eye the pair would make away with every walnut or hazel-nut, every dried raisin, every bit of sugar, which remained. Nothing could be droller than the eager and furtive glances which they cast about them while doing this, or their look of surprise when they found themselves on the edge of the table-cloth. When a tiny board was laid from the cage to the table, they would joyfully run across it and store their plunder away in their private cupboard.

The couple multiplied rapidly, until whole families of equal whiteness ascended and descended the staircases of the cage. At last we found ourselves at the head of thirty rats, all so much at home with us that when the weather was cold they burrowed in our pockets without the least ceremony, and lay there, keeping themselves warm. Sometimes leaving open the door of the Ratopolis, we would go up to the second floor of the house, and give a whistle well known to our pupils. Then the tiny crew, who with great difficulty could climb from one step of the stairs to the other, would swarm upward, clutching the rail, pulling themselves along by the balusters, following each other in a file with the regularity of acrobats, up the steep road, down which occasionally one slipped, and run to find us, uttering little cries and manifesting the liveliest joy.

We must now confess to an act of brutality. We had so often heard it said that a rat's tail resembled a pink worm and detracted from the beauty of the animal, that at last we selected one from our menagerie, and cut off the much-abused appendage. The little rat bore the operation well, grew up bravely, and became a master rat, with a fine pair of moustaches; but in spite of being lightened of the weight of his caudal extremity, he was always less agile than his companions, was wary in gymnastic exercises, and frequently experienced a tumble. When the troop ran up the staircase, he invariably came last; and he always had the air of an acrobat who is testing his tight-rope and is not quite sure of his balance. This experiment convinced us of the usefulness of a tail to rats. It holds them in equilibrium as they run along cornices and narrow projections. When they swiftly turn to right or left the tail turns too, serving as a counterpoise; and this is the cause of the perpetual wiggle which characterizes it. Nature seldom makes a superfluous thing, and for this reason we should be very cautious in trying to improve her handiwork.

You will doubtless wonder how our rats and cats, creatures so totally unsympathetic, — one in fact being the natural prey of the other, — managed to live together. In the most amicable way imaginable. The cats never showed their claws to the rats; the rats never exhibited the least fear or distrust of the cats. This conduct on the part of the cats was thoroughly sincere, and never once were the rats called upon to mourn the death of a comrade. Don Pierrot de Navarre showed the tenderest affection for these tiny neighbors. He would lie down by the cage for hours together, watching them at play. If by accident the door of the room was shut, he would scratch and softly mew to have it opened, that he might rejoin his little white friends, who not infrequently would come from their cage and go to sleep by his side. Seraphita, of a loftier nature than he, and not so fond of the musky odor of rats, never took part in these games; but she did the rats no harm, and suffered them to pass before her without once extending a claw.

The end of these rats was strange enough. One sultry day in summer when the thermometer marked the ordinary heat of Senegal, their cage was placed in the garden, under the shade of a vine-covered arbor; for they seemed to suffer from the heat. A heavy storm came up, with great gusts of wind, lightning and rain. The tall poplars on the river's bank bent like reeds. Armed with an umbrella, we were on the point of going out to look for our pets, when a vivid lightning flash, which seemed to split the very depths of the heavens, stopped us on the first step of the flight which led from the terrace to the garden. A tremendous thunder-clap followed, louder than the discharge of a hundred cannon. The shock was so violent that we were almost thrown down by it.

After this explosion the storm grew a little calmer; and hastening to the arbor we found the thirty-two rats lying with their paws in the air, all killed by the same thunderbolt.

The wire of their cage had without doubt attracted the lightning. Thus perished together, as they had lived together, thirty-two Norway rats, — an enviable death, and one not often granted by implacable fate!

THE BLACK DYNASTY.

CHAPTER III.

DON PIERROT de Navarre, being a native of Havana, needed a very warm temperature. This temperature was provided for him in our rooms; but about the house lay extensive gardens, separated by wire fences which offered no difficulties to a cat, and which were planted with large trees, in whose branches innumerable birds twittered and sang. Not infrequently Pier-rot, profiting by an open door, would make his escape of evenings for the enjoyment of a private hunt over the lawns and the flower-beds wet with dew. Sometimes he had to wait till daylight before he could re-enter the house; for, though he mewed under the windows, his signal did not always rouse the sleepers within. His chest had always been delicate, and one chilly night he took a cold, which speedily developed into consumption. Poor Pierrot! he became painfully thin after a year of coughing. His fur, once so silky, lost its gloss, and reminded one of the dull, opaque whiteness of a winding-sheet. His great transparent eyes looked enormous by contrast with his poor little face. His pink nose grew pale, and he dragged his feet slowly along his favorite sunshiny wall, watching the yellow autumn leaves whirled along in spiral flights by the wind, and looking as though he were repeating to himself the elegy of Millevoye.

There is nothing in the world more touching than a sick animal. It submits to its sufferings with such a sweet, sad resignation. Everything possible was done to save Pierrot. He had a skilful doctor,

who stethoscoped him and felt his pulse.
Asses' milk was ordered, and the poor
thing lapped it willingly enough from his
little porcelain saucer. He would lie for
long hours on our knees, stretched out,
and immovable as the shadow of a sphinx.
We could number his vertebræ with our
fingers, like the beads of a rosary. When
he tried to respond to our caresses by
a feeble mew, it sounded like a death-
rattle. On the day of his death, as he lay
panting upon his side, he raised himself
with a supreme effort and crept toward
us, opening wide his dilated eyes with a
look which seemed to claim our help with
an intense supplication. It said plainly as
words could say, " Come, save me, thou
who art a man !" Then he staggered ; his
eyes became fixed ; and he fell with a cry
so desperate, so lamentable, so full of an-
guish, that we sat transfixed with silent
horror. He was buried at the bottom of

the garden, under a white-rose tree which still marks the place of his grave.

Two or three years later Seraphita died also, of a mysterious disease against which all the resources of science proved unavailing. She is buried not far from Pierrot.

With them the *Dynastie Blanche* became extinct, but not the family. For of this couple, white as snow, were born three kittens as black as ink. Explain, who can, this mystery. The great excitement of the day was Victor Hugo's novel " Les Miserables." No one spoke of anything else, and the names of its heroes and heroines were in every mouth. Naturally, therefore, the two male kittens were christened Enjolras and Gavroche, while their sister received the title of Eponine. When very young they acquired a number of pretty tricks. Among the rest they were taught to run like a dog after a ball made of rolled-up paper, and to fetch it back when thrown to a distance. Even though the ball were tossed up to the cornices of the wardrobes, hidden behind piles of sheets on a shelf, or dropped into a deep vase, they would always discover and fetch it safely in their paws. Later in life they learned to despise these frivolous amusements, and acquired that calm and dreamy philosophy which is the true characteristic of the cat nature.

When people first land in one of the Southern States of America, the negroes they see are to them simply negroes; they cannot tell one from another. So to careless eyes three black cats are three black cats, and nothing more. Observant persons, however, do not make such mistakes. The physiognomies of animals differ from each other like those of men; and we never had the least difficulty in distinguishing between these three faces, all black as the

mask of Harlequin, and lighted by emerald
disks with reflections of gold.

Enjolras, by far the prettiest of the three
cats, could be identified by his large and
lion-like head, his well-whiskered cheeks,
strong shoulders, long back, and a superb
tail which expanded like a plume. There
was something theatrical and emphatic
about him, and he was addicted to *poses*
like a favorite actor. His slow and un-
dulating movements were full of majesty.
He could be trusted to walk over consoles
loaded with treasures in china and Venice
glass, so circumspectly did he order his
footsteps. He was not much of a Stoic
in character, and his taste for dainties
would have horrified his namesake Enjolras, that sober and pure young man, who
would doubtless have said to him, as the
angel did to Swedenborg, " Thou eatest
too much." This gluttonous turn, which
was as droll as that of a gastronomic

monkey, was indulged; and Enjolras attained a size and weight most unusual in a domestic cat. The idea occurred to us to have him shaved like a poodle, in order to complete his resemblance to a lion. A mane was left to him, and one thick tuft of hair at the end of his tail. We will not swear that it was not part of the original design to furnish him with leg-of-mutton whiskers like those in the portrait of Munito. Thus accoutred, he looked, it must be confessed, less like a lion of the jungle or of the Cape than like a Japanese chimera. Never was a more absurd whim carried out upon the body of a living animal. His hair was shaved so closely that it showed the skin, which exhibited odd bluish tones, and contrasted in the most extraordinary way with the blackness of his mane.

Gavroche, as if to suit with the character of his namesake in the novel, was a cat of a crafty and furtive disposition. Smaller than Enjolras, his agility was most comical and surprising. His substitutes for the jokes and slang of the Paris *gamin* were capers, somersaults, and ludicrous motions. We are forced to confess that, notwithstanding these attractive qualities, Gavroche never lost an opportunity of stealing out of the parlor in order to join in the street or courtyard with vagabond cats, —

"Of any sort of birth, and blood unknown to fame,"

in parties of the most unrefined sort, quite forgetting his dignity as a cat from Havana: son of the illustrious Don Pierrot de Navarre, grandee of Spain of the first rank, and of the Marquise Seraphita, whose manners were so lofty and disdainful. Sometimes by way of a treat he would conduct to his porridge-plate some comrade emaciated by famine and all skin-and-bone, whom he had picked up during

his peregrinations; introducing him with
all the airs of a condescending prince.
The poor wretch, with drooping ears,
sidelong glance, and tail between his legs,
fearing that his free lunch might at any
moment be interrupted by the housemaid's
broom, would gobble down double, triple,
quadruple mouthfuls, and like *Siete-Aguas,*
or Seven Waters, of the Spanish *posada,*
make the plate in a few seconds as clean
as though it had been scrubbed by a
Dutch housewife to serve as a model to
Mieris or Gerard Dow.

Beholding these chosen protégés of Gavroche's, that phrase with which Gavarni
illustrates one of his caricatures frequently
came into our head: "Fine friends these
are which you have selected to go about
with!" But after all they were only a
proof of Gavroche's real goodness of heart;
for he might easily have eaten up everything himself.

The cat who bore the name of the interesting Eponine was more slender and delicately made than her brothers. Her nose was slightly longer; her eyes set obliquely in the head like those of a Chinese, were of a green hue like the eyes of Pallas Athene, to which Homer invariably applies the epithet γλαυκῶπις. Her nose of a velvety blackness, as finely grained as a Perigord truffle; her moustaches perpetually waving, made up a physiognomy full of expression. Her superb black fur was always in a quiver, and glittered with changeful lustres. Never was there a creature so sympathetic, nervous, and theatrical as Eponine. If you passed your hand over her back once or twice in the dusk little blue sparks would flash from the fur. Eponine attached herself to us as devotedly as did the Eponine of the novel to Marius; but not being pre-occupied with a Cosette, as was that dear young

man, we were able to respond to the affection of this tender and devoted cat,
who is still the companion of our labors
and the joy of our suburban hermitage.
At the sound of the door-bell she runs
out, receives the visitors, shows them into
the drawing-room, asks them to sit down,
talks with them; yes, *talks*, prattling on
with murmurs and little cries which are
not in the least like those which cats
use to one another, but which resemble
the speech of men. What does she say,
do you ask? She says in the most intel-
ligible language: " Gentlemen and ladies,
do not be impatient; look at the pictures,
or, if you please, converse with me. Monsieur will be here soon." When we enter
she discreetly retires to an easy chair or
the corner of the piano, and listens to
the conversation without trying to take
part in it, like a polite animal who is
familiar with the habits of good society.

This charming Eponine has given so many proofs of merit, of intelligence, and superior social qualities, that by common consent she has been elevated to the dignity of a *person;* for there can be no doubt that her conduct is governed by a reason which is far superior to instinct. This dignity gives her the right to eat at table like a human being, and not as cats do out of a saucer set on the floor in a corner. Eponine therefore has her chair, which is regularly placed beside our own, at breakfast and dinner. In consideration of her shape and size, leave is given her to place her fore-paws on the edge of the table. She has also her own plate and her own tumbler, but not a fork or spoon. She watches the dinner through all its courses from soup to dessert, waiting for her turn to be helped, and altogether comporting herself with a wisdom and decency which we wish that children

LEAVE IS GIVEN HER TO PLACE HER FOREPAWS ON
THE EDGE OF THE TABLE.

would oftener imitate. At the first tinkle
of the bell she makes her appearance, and
when we enter the dining-room there she
is, already seated on her chair with her
paws crossed before her on the edge of
the table; and she holds up her forehead
to be kissed precisely as a nice little girl
does who has been trained to show an
affectionate politeness towards her parents
and other elderly friends.

But there are flaws in the diamond,
spots even on the sun, shadows upon perfection, and Eponine, it must be owned,
has an over-passionate love for fish, — a
passion which is shared by cats in general.
In contradiction to the Latin proverb

"Catus amat pisces, sed non vult tingere plantas,"

she will dip her paw into water without the
least hesitation in order to draw out a carp,
a white bait, or a trout. Fish awake in her
a sort of frenzy; and like children who are

in a state of excitement over the idea
of dessert, she sometimes looks sulkily at
the soup, when preliminary observations
made in the kitchen have assured her
that there is fish to come, and that the
cook has no need to expiate a failure by
falling on his sword, as did the noble
Vatel.   At such times she is left un-
served, and we say to her coldly, "*Mademoiselle*, a *person* who is not hungry for
soup cannot be hungry for fish," and
the dish is carried pitilessly past under
her very nose.   When matters reach this
serious stage the dainty Eponine gobbles
up her soup in all haste to the very last
drop, despatches every crumb of bread or
Italian paste, and then turns round and
looks at us with a proud glance as one who
has done her duty, and whose conscience is
henceforth free from reproach.   Her por-
tion of fish is then given her.   She eats
it with the utmost satisfaction, and having

tasted of all the other dishes, finishes her meal with a glass of water.

When a dinner-party is projected Eponine, without seeing the guests, understands perfectly well that there is to be company that evening. She takes a look at her usual place, and, if she notices a knife, fork, and spoon beside the plate, she decamps without a word and seats herself on the piano-stool, which is her chosen refuge on such occasions. I should be glad if people who deny the possession of reason to animals, would explain this fact, apparently so simple and yet containing such a world of inferences. From seeing beside her plate those utensils which man only can use, this wise and observant cat argues that, for the day, she must yield her place to a guest, and she makes haste to do so. She never deceives herself about the matter, but sometimes, when the visitor is one with whom she is on familiar terms, she will climb his knee and try to coax a few tit-bits out of him by her grace and caresses.

But enough of this; we must not weary our readers. Stories about cats are less popular than those about dogs. Still, we feel obliged to tell the end of Enjolras and Gavroche. In some text-books there is this sentence: "Sua eum perdidit ambitio." One might say of Enjolras, "Sua eum perdidit pinguetudo" — he died of his own fat. He was mistaken for a hare and killed by some idiotic hunters. His murderers, however, perished within a twelvemonth, and in the most miserable manner. The death of a black cat, that most cabalistical of creatures, never goes unavenged!

Gavroche, seized with a fanatical love of liberty, or perhaps with sudden madness, leaped out of a window one day, crossed the street, climbed the high fence surrounding St. James' Church, which stands opposite our house, and disappeared. In spite of our anxious enquiries no traces of him could ever be found. A mysterious shadow hovers over his fate. Thus of the black dynasty only Eponine remains. She is faithful still to her master, and to all intents and purposes has become an educated cat.

She has for companion a magnificent Angora, of a silver-gray coat which makes one think of clouded Chinese porcelain. His name is Zizi, which means — " Too handsome to do anything." This beautiful creature lives in a sort of contemplative stupor like a *thekiari* during his period of inebriation. Looking at him one is reminded of the "Ecstasies of M. Hochener." Zizi's passion is music. Not content with listening to it, he is himself a performer. Occasionally at night when all are sleeping there breaks upon the silence a strange, fantastic melody which Kriesler and the musicians of the future might well envy. It is Zizi, walking up and down the keyboard of the piano and enjoying the rapture of hearing the notes sing under his feet.

It would be unfair not to give a passing mention to Cleopatra, the daughter of Eponine, who is a charming animal, but of too timid a nature to be introduced to the public. She is of a deep fawn color, like Mummia, the shaggy companion of Atta Croll, and her dark green eyes are just like two enormous pieces of aqua-marina. She walks habitually on three paws, and holds the fourth in the air, like the figure of a classical line which has lost his marble ball.

This then is the chronicle of the Black Dynasty, — Enjolras, Gavroche, Eponine, — recalling to us the creations of a beloved master. Only, when we now glance over

" Les Miserables," it seems as though the principal characters in the romance are taken by black cats, but this fact does not in the least diminish the interest of the story for us.

CHAPTER IV.

OUR DOGS.

WE have sometimes been accused of disliking dogs. This at first sight does not seem to be a very grave charge, still, we feel bound to justify ourselves, since the accusation carries with it a certain amount of disgrace. People who prefer cats to dogs, pass in the eyes of most persons as necessarily false, voluptuous and cruel; while dog-lovers are supposed to be invariably pure, loyal, open characters, gifted, in short, with all the attributes which are popularly ascribed to the canine race. We could in no wise detract from the merits of Medor, Turc, Merot, and other equally amiable beasts, and we are quite ready to agree with the maxim formulated

OUR DOGS.

by Charlet: "The best thing which a man possesses is his dog." We have owned many, we still own some; and if our calumniators will kindly call at our residence they will be greeted by the shrill and furious barking of a small Cuban lap-dog, and by a large greyhound who will take much pleasure in biting their ankles.

Still, we will not deny that our liking for dogs has a strong admixture of fear. These animals, excellent, faithful, devoted as they are, may at any moment run mad, and in that condition they are as dangerous and deadly as the viper, the asp, the bell-serpent, or the cobra di capello. This thought somewhat moderates our raptures over them. But, apart from this, dogs somehow produce a disquieting effect upon us. Their eyes are so deep, so intense; they place themselves before us with such an interrogative air that it is almost embarrassing. Goethe did not like,

any more than ourselves, this gaze which
seems to assimilate a man's most secret
thoughts. He would drive the poor animals away, and say to them " You have
done your best : you shall not devour my
identity."

The Pharamond of our canine dynasty
was named Luther. He was a large white
pointer with red spots, and handsome
brown ears, who, having lost his master,
and searched after him vainly for a long
time, domesticated himself in the house
of our parents, who then lived at Passy.
Having no partridges to hunt he gave
himself up to the pursuit of rats, in which
pursuit he became as proficient as a Scotch
terrier. At that time we were living in a
room in that blind alley of Doyennè, no
longer in existence, where Gérard de Ner-
val, Arséne Houssaye, and Camille Rogier
had established themselves as the centres
of a picturesque little Bohemian circle of

artists and literary men, whose freaks and eccentricities have been too often described elsewhere to need further mention now. There, in the very midst of the Carrousel, we lived a life as free and as lonely as if in some desert isle of the ocean,—among nettles and blocks of stone, under the shadow of the Louvre, and close to the ruins of an old church, whose crumbling arches presented the most picturesque effects by moonlight. Luther, with whom we had always been on friendly terms, seeing us thus take our final flight from the family nest, assumed the task of making us a daily visit. He left Passy each morning at some time unknown, and, following the Quai de Billy and the Cours-la-Reine, arrived about eight o'clock, just as we were waking up. Scratching at the door, which was always opened for him, he threw himself upon us with a joyous yelping, put his fore-paws on our

knees, received with great simplicity and
modesty the caresses which his good conduct had earned, made a rapid inspection
of the room, and then set out on his
homeward journey.   Arrived at Passy,
he would at once run to our mother,
wagging his tail and uttering little barks
which said as plainly as words, " Do not
be anxious, I have seen the young master,
and he is well."   Having thus given a re-
port of his self-imposed mission he would
lap a bowl full of water, eat his porridge,
and, stretching himself near the easy chair
of mamma, for whom he had a particular
affection, would refresh himself by an hour
or two of sleep after the long journey that
he had taken.

Those who hold that animals do not
think and are incapable of putting two
ideas together, may explain as best they
can this daily visit which kept up the
family relations, and gave to the old birds

in the nest regular news of their recently escaped fledgling.

Poor Luther! he had a melancholy end. He gradually became silent and morose, and one day fled from the house, apparently because he felt himself attacked by hydrophobia and feared that he might be led to bite his master. We have every reason to suppose that he was killed as a mad dog. At all events we never saw him again.

After rather a long interval, a new dog was installed at the house — a dog called Zamore. He was half mongrel, half spaniel, small in size, and with a black coat, excepting for a few spots of flame color beneath his eyebrows and some tones of fawn color on the belly. He was, in short, insignificant in appearance and rather ugly than pretty, but so far as moral qualities are concerned he was really a remarkable dog. For women he had an absolute contempt; he would neither follow nor obey them, and our mother and our sisters tried in vain to win from him the least evidence of friendship or respect. He would loftily accept their attentions and their tit-bits, but he never deigned to give them a word of thanks in return. No barking for them, no drumming of his tail against the floor, none of those endearments of which dogs are so prodigal. Toward these he maintained always an attitude impassive and impassible, crouching in the position of a sphinx, like some serious and dignified personage who disdains to mix in a frivolous conversation.

The master he elected to serve was our father whom he recognized in the head of the family and a man of weight and character. Zamore's tenderness, even for him, was of an austere and stoical sort, and never expressed by merriment, or antics, or lickings of the tongue.

But his eyes were forever fixed on his master, his head turned to watch each slightest movement, and everywhere he followed him, his nose close to his master's heel, never permitting himself to play the smallest prank, or paying the least attention to any dog whom they met. This dear and lamented father of ours was a great fisher before the Lord. The barbels caught by him must have out-numbered the antelopes caught by Nimrod. It could never be said of his fishing-rod that it was an instrument with a hook at one end and a fool at the other, for he was a man full of wit and intelligence, which, however, did not hinder his filling his fish-basket every day. Zamore always accompanied him on these excursions, and during those long nocturnal watchings, which are necessary for the capture of such fish as only bite when the line touches bottom, he would place himself close to the water's edge and seem to explore the darksome depths with his eyes, as if searching for the prey. Though he now and then pricked up his ears at those numberless vague and distant sounds which are audible even in the deepest silence of the night, he never uttered a bark, for he perfectly understood that it is indispensable for a fisherman's dog to be dumb. Diana might lift her alabaster brow above the horizon and the river give back the reflection; it was all in vain; not even at the moon would Zamore bark, though such midnight bayings are among the chief pleasures of animals of his species. Only when the bell on the fishing-line tinkled did he indulge in a yelp, for then he knew that the prey was secured, and he took intense interest in those after manœuvres which are requisite for landing a barbel of three or four pounds weight.

Who could have guessed that under

this calm and self-contained exterior, so philosophical, so far removed from all frivolity, lurked one imperious and extravagant passion, in utter contradiction to the apparent character, moral and physical, of this animal so serious and so thoughtful that one would have almost called him sad?

What, you say, has this admirable Zamore then some hidden vice? No. Was he a thief, a libertine? No. Had he a taste for brandy-cherries? No. Did he bite? Ten thousand times, no! Zamore's passion was for dancing. In him, a true Terpsichorean artist was lost to the world.

This vocation was discovered in the following manner. One day there appeared in the public square at Passy a grayish ass, one of those luckless donkeys belonging to a juggler, which Decamps and Fouquet have so successfully painted.

Two panniers, balanced across his galled
back, held a troop of trained dogs, cos-
tumed according to sex as marquises,
troubadours, Turks, Swiss shepherds, and
queens of Golconda. The show-man lifted
out the dogs, cracked his whip, and instantly all the actors exchanged the hori-
zontal position for the perpendicular, and
transformed themselves from quadrupeds
into bipeds. A fife and a tambourine
sounded, and the ballet began.

Zamore, who was strolling gravely past,
stopped short, astonished at the spectacle.
These gayly caparisoned dogs, with laced
seams and clinking ornaments, plumed
hats and turbans on their heads, and such
an odd resemblance to men and women,
seemed to him supernatural beings. Their
measured steps, their courtesies, their *pi-
rouettes* enchanted but did not discourage
him. Like Correggio before the pictures
of Raphael, he cried in the canine lan-

guage, "Anch' io son pittore," " I also am a painter," and, seized with noble emulation as the troop defiled before him in a ladies' chain, he raised himself on his hind legs which visibly shook, and, to the vociferous delight of the bystanders, made a movement to join them. But the showman was not so much charmed as the bystanders. He gave Zamore a sharp cut of his whip and drove him from the circle, just as one might expel from the door of a theatre a spectator who, during the progress of the play, took it into his head to climb on to the stage and join in the ballet.

This public humiliation, however, did not deter Zamore from following his vocation. He ran back to the house with his tail between his legs and an air of deep thought. All that day he was more silent, pre-occupied and morose than usual. That night our two little sisters were roused from their sleep by a low, mysterious noise which seemed to come from an unoccupied chamber next to their own, where Zamore was in the habit of passing the night on an old arm-chair. The sound was a sort of rhythmic stamping, which in the quiet of the night sounded louder than it really was. At first the children thought that it must be the mice giving a ball, but the steps and the jumps were too loud and heavy for mice. At last the bravest of the two crept out of bed, half opened the door, and peeped in. What did she see by the light of a struggling moonbeam but Zamore, erect on his hind legs, beating time with his fore-paws, and practising as in a dancing class the steps which he had so much admired that morning in the street. Monsieur was studying his lesson !

This was not, as might be supposed, a random fancy, pursued for one night only.

MONSIEUR WAS STUDYING HIS LESSON.

Zamore persisted in his Terpsichorean
aspirations, and in time became an admirable dancer. Every day, as soon as the
fife and the tambourine began to sound,
he ran to the square, glided between the
legs of the spectators, and with the deepest
attention watched the trained dogs going
through with their exercises. Mindful,
however, of that cut of the whip, he
never again tried to join in the dance,
but, noting carefully each step, each movement, each graceful attitude, rehearsed it
at night in the privacy of his own room,—
while by day he maintained his usual aus-
terity of demeanor. After a time, to imitate no longer sufficed him; he began to
invent, to compose new steps, and we are
bound to say that few dogs have ever sur-
passed him in this noble accomplishment.

We ourselves, concealed behind the half-
open door, have often watched him at his
practice. He put so much energy and

fire into his exercise that, morning after morning, the huge bowl of water set for his refreshment in the corner of the room the night before would be found drained of every drop.

At length the day came when, all his difficulties conquered, he felt himself the equal of any four-legged dancer in creation, and now it seemed only proper to remove the bushel which had hitherto obscured his candle, and give the world the benefit of his talents.

The courtyard of the house was closed on one side by a grating which had openings wide enough to allow of the passage of dogs of an ordinary size. One morning fifteen or twenty such friends of Zamore's — connoisseurs, without doubt, to whom he had sent cards of invitation for his debut in the choregraphic art — were noticed assembling round a level square of earth (which the artist seemed to have swept

WHEN PAYING LITTLE ATTENTIONS TO HIS LADY-LOVES
HE STOOD ALWAYS ON HIS HIND-LEGS.

clean with his tail), and the performances commenced. The audience was enthusiastic, and manifested its approbation with bow-wows which sounded extremely like the " Bravos ! " of opera-goers. With the exception of one old water-spaniel of a muddy and degraded appearance, who seemed an adverse critic, and yelped out something about "sound traditions ignored and forgotten," all united in pronouncing Zamore the Vestris of dogs and the true genius of the dance. A minuet, a jig, and a waltz *à deux temps* were included in the programme. Quite a number of two-legged spectators joined the four-legged ones before the entertainment was concluded, and Zamore had the honor and satisfaction of being applauded by the clapping of human hands.

After this his habits became so entirely those of the dancer that, when paying casual attentions to his lady-loves, he stood

always on his hind legs, making courteous
little bows and turning out his toes like
a gallant marquis of the *ancien régime;*
nothing was lacking but the plumed opera-
hat under the arm.

Except for these occasional interludes
Zamore's character was as splenetic as
that of other comic actors, and he took
no share whatever in the ordinary life of
the house. He never stirred except when
he saw his master take his hat and cane,
and he died finally of brain fever, caused, as
we supposed, by the over-exertion and excitement of learning the *Schottische,* which
just then came into fashion. From his grave
Zamore might say, like the Greek dancer
in the epitaph, " Lie on me lightly, earth,
for I have very lightly weighed on thee."

Some may ask why, with such remarkable talents, Zamore was not engaged as
one of the troupe of M. Corvi. Even
then we had sufficient influence as a critic

to negotiate such an arrangement had it been desirable. But Zamore would not leave his master; he sacrificed his self-love to his love, — a devotion which one cannot hope very often to find among men.

Our dancer was replaced by a singer named Kobold, — a King Charles spaniel of the purest breed, brought from the famous kennels of Lord Lauder. Nothing earthly was ever so like a chimera as this droll little creature, with his enormous, bulging forehead, his prominent eyes, his nose which seemed broken off at the base, and his long ears which swept the ground. Carried over to France, Kobold, who spoke only English, seemed at first to be half-stupefied. The orders given were perfectly unintelligible to him. Trained to obey " Go on," " Come here," he stood motionless and perplexed at the sound of " Va " and " Va-t'en."

It took him a year to learn the language

of his new country well enough to be able to join in conversation. Kobold was very sensitive to music, and sang several little songs himself, though with a strong English accent. The key-note was given him on the piano, he caught the exact tone, and in a flute-like and sighing voice warbled passages which were really musical, and bore no relation whatever to barkings or yelpings.

When we wanted him to begin again it was only necessary to say, "Sing a little more," and he at once recommenced the cadence. For a creature brought up in the most delicate luxury, and with all the care which one would naturally give to a tenor and a gentleman of distinction, Kobold had the most singular tastes. He devoured earth like a Digger Indian; and this habit, of which he could not be cured, brought on a disease of which he died. He had a strong turn for grooms, horses,

and stables in general, and our ponies had
no comrade more devoted than he. In
fact, he may be said to have divided his
time between the box-stalls and the piano.
From Kobold, the King Charles, we pass
to Myrza, a small Cuban lap-dog, who at
one time had the honor to belong to Giula
Grisi, from whom we received her as a
present. She is white as snow, especially
when freshly washed, and before she has
had time to roll in the dust, — a mania
which some dogs share with a certain kind
of dusty-winged birds. She is the gentlest
of animals, very demonstrative, and guile-
less as a dove. Nothing can be droller
than her shaggy head, her face composed
of two eyes as glittering as furniture nails,
and a little nose which might easily be
mistaken for a Piedmont truffle. Long
locks of hair, as curly as Astrakan wool,
fly about this nose in picturesque confu-
sion, sometimes getting into one eye, some-

times into the other, — the whole making up the most whimsical countenance imaginable, as odd and as unreal as the face of a chameleon.

In Myrza's case nature has imitated art with such perfection that any one would be ready to swear that she came straight from the show-case of a toy-shop. With her blue collar, silver bell, and her hair of the regulation frizz, she looks exactly like a pasteboard dog; and when she barks, one instinctively examines her feet to see if there is not a tiny squeaking-machine fastened under the paws.

Myrza, who spends three quarters of the day in sleep, so that life would seem pretty much the same to her if she were in reality stuffed, and who under ordinary circumstances is anything but bright, nevertheless gave one day a proof of intelligence such as we have never known in any other dog. Bonnegrace, who painted those portraits of Tchoumakoff and of M. E. H., — which were so much talked about when exhibited, had brought a portrait for us to look at, painted after the style of Pagnest, which is so full of vivid color and lifelike light and shadow. Although we have always lived in such intimate relations with animals, and could cite hundreds of instances in which cats, dogs, and birds have proved themselves wise, philosophical, and ingenious, we are forced to admit that the taste for art is totally lacking among them. We have never seen an animal who took the slightest notice of a picture, and the story of the birds who pecked at the grapes painted by Apelles has always appeared to us a pure invention. The one essential distinction between man and beast seems to be just this sense of art and feeling for decoration. A dog would be as likely to put on earrings, as to waste time over pictures.

Well, Myrza, catching sight of Bonne-grace's portrait set up against the wall, jumped from the stool where she was lying rolled up like a ball, rushed to the canvas, and began to bark furiously, trying to bite the intrusive stranger who had entered the room. Her surprise was extreme when she recognized the fact that she had a flat surface to deal with, on which her teeth made no impression, and which was only a deceitful show. She smelt the picture, tried in vain to get behind the frame, looked at us both with a questioning expression in her eyes, and then went back to the stool and resumed her nap, taking no further trouble about the gentleman in oil-colors. Her own countenance, meanwhile, will not be lost to posterity, for a beautiful portrait of her is in existence, painted by M. Victor Madarasz, an Hungarian artist.

We will conclude our chapter on dogs

with the history of Dash. One day a rag-and-bottle man stopped at our door in search of scraps of broken glass and old bottles. In his cart was a puppy some three or four months old, which he had been told to drown, — an order which troubled the honest fellow, at whom the puppy was casting tender and supplicating looks, as if he understood the situation of affairs. The reason of the severe sentence passed on the poor brute was that one of his fore-paws was broken.

Pity stirred in our heart, and we adopted the condemned victim on the spot. A veterinary surgeon was sent for, who set the leg and put it in splints; but Dash persisted in gnawing off the bandages, so that the bones did not unite, and the paw remained dangling uselessly, like the sleeve of a man who has lost his arm. This infirmity, however, did not hinder Dash from being one of the gayest, liveliest, and most alert of dogs; and he ran on three legs quite as fast as was desirable.

He was the commonest of street dogs, a veritable mongrel, on whose breed Buffon himself would have been embarrassed to decide. He was ugliness personified, but possessed an expressive face, which sparkled with intelligence. Everything that was said to him he understood,— his expression changing according as the words, spoken in the same tone of voice, were flattering or abusive. He rolled his eyes, turned up his chops, abandoned himself to unrestrained, nervous wriggles, or laughed, showing a row of white teeth; and, in short, produced the most comical effect, of which he was quite conscious. Very often he tried to speak. With paws placed upon our knee, he would eye us with an intense look, and begin a series of murmurs, sighs, and growls, so varied in intonation that it was easy to see that they were parts of a regular language. Now and then, in the midst of this conversation, Dash would in-terject a sudden and noisy yelp. Then we would look severely at him, and say: " That is barking, not talking. Can it be that after all you are only an animal?" Whereupon Dash, much humiliated by the insinuation, would recommence his vocal-ization, throwing into it a still more pa-thetic expression. No one could doubt that at these times he was giving an ac-count of his misfortunes.

Dash adored sugar. He always came in with the coffee after dessert, and went round the table begging a lump of sugar from each person with an urgency which seldom failed of success. In the end he grew to consider these benevolent gifts in the light of a regular tax, which he rigor-ously exacted. This cur, in the body of a Thersites, carried the soul of an Achilles. Disabled as he was, he constantly attacked, with the frenzy of an heroic courage, dogs ten times as big as himself, and was frightfully beaten. Like Don Quixote, the brave knight of La Mancha, he set out in triumph, and came back in most piteous plight. Alas, he fell a victim to this mistaken courage. He was brought home, a few months since, torn to pieces by an amiable brute of a Newfoundland, who the very next day broke the backbone of a greyhound.

The death of Dash was followed by all sorts of catastrophes. The mistress of the house in which he had received his death-blow was burned to death in her bed a few days after; and her husband, in trying to save her, met with the same fate. It was not an expiation, it was only a fatal coincidence, — for they were the best people in the world, loving animals like Brahmins, and not in the least to blame for the sad fate of our poor Dash.

We have now another dog, who is called Nero, but he is too recent an acquisition to have a history.

In the next chapter we propose to give a chronicle of the different chameleons, lizards, magpies, and other small creatures who have made part of our household of pets.

N. B. Alas, Nero is dead! He was poisoned a day or two since as thoroughly as if he had supped with the Borgias, and the first chapter of his life begins and ends with an epitaph.

CHAPTER V.

CHAMELEONS, LIZARDS, AND MAGPIES.

ONCE upon a time we happened to be at the port of Santa-Maria in the Bay of Cadiz, a little village which seems cut out of the white loaf of Spain, between the indigo of the sea and the lapis-lazuli of the sky. It was noon, and on that particular day such a warm noon that the sun appeared to be amusing himself by dropping spoonfuls of melted lead on the heads of travellers, as the garrison of a beleaguered fortress, by some well-planned artifice, pours boiling oil or pitch on the heads of its assailants. This picturesque little port is made famous by the celebrated song in the Andalusian *patois* of

THE CHAMELEON.

Murillo-Bravo, " The Bulls of Puerto," in which the gallant boatman says to the lady about to embark, " Lleve V. la patita." We hummed the refrain in a voice which sings no less falsely in Spanish than in French, following with our eyes, as we sang, the line, straight as the selvage of a piece of linen, which was cast by the shadow at the foot of the wall.

It was a market day, and foreign commodities of all sorts were exposed for sale on the square, which were of colors gorgeous enough to enchant Ziem himself. Garlands of fiery-red peppers swung above deep-green melons, some of which had been cut in halves to show the rose-colored pulp within, dotted with black spots like a shell from the South Seas. Heavy clusters of clear, yellow grapes, like amber beads, reminding one by their fair transparency of Turkish rosaries, hung by the side of bunches of a bluish color, and

others which were of an amethystine hue
shading into deeper purple. Chickpeas
in weedy mats rounded their globes of
paly gold; pomegranates, bursting their
rinds, showed caskets of rubies within.
The fruit-sellers, with their scarlet and yellow capes, their black silk petticoats, bare
feet thrust into satin slippers, — and what
feet, hardly bigger than a Savoy biscuit!
— their paper fans held against the cheek
to take the place of a parasol, sat proudly
beside their vegetables chattering with that
Andalusian volubility which is so full of
grace.   Here and there some passing gallant, balancing himself on the point of his
white cane, his jacket swinging from his
shoulders, a broad sash from Gibraltar en-
circling his waist from armpit to hips, his
elastic breeches open at the knee, and
leathern boots from Ronda unbuttoned all
the way up the leg, in what seems to be
the height of the style, lingered a moment

to cast a seductive glance while rolling between thumb and forefinger his ciga-rette of alcoy paper. It was one of those blinding effects of southern light and color which would be called an exaggeration of nature if any artist should attempt to reproduce in full its crude and dazzling truth.

We sought a refuge from the fiery sun shower in the *patio* of The Three Moorish Kings. A patio, as all the world knows, is an inside court surrounded by arcades, whose arrangement reminds one of the ancient *impluvium.* In place of a roof it is shaded by a linen awning striped with gay colors, called in Spanish a *velarium,* which is kept constantly wet, in order to secure greater coolness. In the middle of this patio a slender thread of water rose and fell from a marble basin, throwing a fine spray over boxes of myrtles, pome-granates and oleanders, which were grouped about it. Sofas covered with horse-hair, and cane-seated chairs, were scattered about under the arcades. Guitars, suspended on the walls, cast brilliant reflections out of the shadow, as the light glinted on their varnished surfaces, and beside them hung the brown disks of tambourines.

These patios are common in the Moorish houses of Algeria, and no better contrivance to secure coolness can be imagined. They are a device of the Arabs adopted by the Spaniards. Upon the capitals of the smaller columns, in many dwellings, can still be read verses from the Koran glorifying Allah, or laudations of some caliph long ago driven back into the heart of Africa and forgotten.

After draining an unglazed jug of cold water we retired to one of the rooms opening on the patio for a siesta. Our drowsy eyes wandered to the ceiling of the low chamber, which, like all Spanish ceilings, was whitewashed, and ornamented in the middle by a rosette picked out into yellow, black, and red sections like the sides of a ball. From this rosette hung a cord meant, without doubt, to hold a lamp; and along this cord a mysterious object was moving upward. We fitted our eye-glass into its place under the arch of our eyebrow, and at last made out that the thing, which with so much pains was climbing on the cord toward the ceiling, was a kind of lizard, of a grayish yellow, and a shape which had about it something monstrous, recalling in miniature those vast Saurians which disappeared from earth at the close of the antediluvian epoch.

The maid of the inn was summoned, — Pepa, Lola, or Casilda, we cannot recall the exact name, but are ready to swear that she was an excellent person, — and she explained that the creature on the cord was a chameleon.

Lola, — if Lola it was, — taking pity on our ignorance, and perhaps not sorry to exhibit her own zoölogical knowledge, said to us in an instructive way, "These animals change their color, you know, according to the place where they happen to be, and they live on air."

During our brief conversation the chameleons (for there were two) continued their ascension of the cord. Nothing more absurd than their appearance could be imagined. It must be admitted that the chameleon is not beautiful, and, although people say that Nature does everything well, it strikes us that by taking a very little more trouble she might easily have made a prettier animal than he. But, like all great artists, Nature has her caprices, and she occasionally amuses herself by modelling grotesque shapes. The eyes of the chameleon, which are almost completely detached from the head, are fitted into external membranous sacs, and have complete independence of movement. They can look to the right with one and to the left with the other, cast one up to the skies and the other down to the floor, producing thereby a variety of squints which have the most extraordinary effect. A swollen pouch under the jaw, not unlike a goitre, gives the poor animal an air of haughty complacency and stupid conceit, of which he is as unconscious as he is innocent. His awkwardly formed paws make a projecting angle above the line of his back, and his movements are alike ungraceful and meaningless.

One of the chameleons had now reached the top of the string and the centre of the rosette. Putting out a pitiful little paw, he tried the ceiling to see if it were possible to cling to it, and in that way to effect an

escape. In making this experiment, for
the hundredth time perhaps, he squinted
with his eyes in the most desperate and
touching way, as if invoking aid from
heaven and earth; then, seeing no hope
of egress on that side, he slowly began
to descend the cord again, with a sad,
resigned, and piteous look, — emblem of
useless labor, a Sisyphus of wasted ener-
gies. Half-way down the two creatures
met, exchanged glances meant to be
friendly, perhaps, but horrible from their
squints, and for a moment or two formed
a group which was like a hideous bunch
on the perpendicular line of the string.

After a few ludicrous contortions the
group disentangled, each chameleon con-
tinuing its journey, the one which was coming down reaching the end of the cord,
stretching out a hind leg, sounding the
air cautiously and finding no place of support, drawing it in again with a discour-

aged movement whose heart-breaking and absurd melancholy baffles all description. By one of those associations of ideas which cannot be accounted for, but which the mind conceives without understanding why, the chameleons reminded me of one of Goya's gloomiest etchings, in which are represented spectres, who, with feeble and shadowy arms, are trying to lift heavy stones which roll back upon and crush them, — an unequal conflict of weakness with destiny.

In order to deliver these poor animals from their sufferings we bought for them a rough sort of cage. It was of good size, and, once installed therein, they were able to dispense with those acrobatic exercises which seemed to make them so miserable. As to the question of food, with all respect for Southern frugality, this living on air by its very name seems insufficient. A Spanish lover may, perhaps, be able to breakfast on a glass of water, dine on a cigarette, and sup on a tune from his mandolin; but the tastes of chameleons are less refined, and they crave and devour flies, which they catch, in the oddest manner, by darting out from the throat a sort of long lance covered with a viscous slime, which adheres to the wings of the insect, and, when drawn in again, carries him bodily along with it into the gullet.

Do chameleons change their color according to the place where they happen to be? In the literal sense of the words they do not, but their skins, broken by little facet-shaped roughnesses, absorb the hues of surrounding objects more easily than other bodies do. Placed near a red thing, or a yellow or a green one, the chameleon seems to steep itself in that color, but, after all, it is but an effect of refraction. A plate of polished metal will be colored in the same way; there is no real power of absorption. In its ordinary state the chameleon is of a gray-green or a yellowish gray. However, those who have a taste for marvels may, if they like, assert that the chameleon changes its color at will, and is thus the proper emblem of political versatility; but we must be permitted to say in our turn that after the minutest observations, continued for a long time, we are convinced that chameleons are entirely indifferent to affairs of state and everything connected with them.

We were anxious to carry our chameleons home with us, but the autumn was near at hand, and, though the sun still had a great deal of heat as we followed the coast northward from Tarifa to Port Vendres, passing by Gibraltar, Malaga, Alicante, Almeria, Valencia, and Barcelona, the poor beasts faded away before our very sight. As they wasted, their eyes seemed to project from their heads, and day by

8

day to increase in prominence. Their squint increased; under their loose and flabby skins their tiny skeletons grew more and more distinct with every mile. It was a piteous sight, — these consumptive lizards feebly going through the death dance, and too weak even to thrust their sticky tongues out for the flies which we collected for them in the galley of the steamer. They died within a few days of each other, and the blue Mediterranean was their grave.

From chameleons to lizards the transition is easy. Our youngest daughter once received the present of a lizard which had been caught at Fontainebleau, and which became very fond of her. Jacques' color was the most beautiful Veronese green that can be imagined. His eyes were very bright, his scales overlapped each other with the most perfect regularity, and his movements were extraordinarily swift. He

never left his little mistress, and usually
lay hidden in a loop of her hair near the
comb. Nestled there, he accompanied her
to the play, to walk, to evening parties,
without once betraying his presence; only,
when the young girl was playing on the
piano, he would desert his retreat, descend
her shoulder and creep out to the end of
the arm, always preferring the right hand,
which plays the air, to the left, which
makes the accompaniment, — thus testify-
ing to his preference for melody over har-
mony.

Jacques' house was a glass box lined
with moss, which had once contained Rus-
sian cigars from the Eliseïeph manufac-
tory. His private life may therefore be
justly said to have lain open to the public.
His food consisted of drops of milk, which
he preferred to take from the end of his
mistress's finger. He died of grief and
hunger during her absence on a journey,

to which she had not dared to expose him on account of the severity of the weather.

There is nothing to be told of Balylas, the sparrow, but that he died. One blow under his wing, from a claw, finished his career, and he was buried in a domino-box.

It now only remains for us to describe Margot, the magpie, — a most intelligent and chatty gossip, worthy to live in an osier cage in the window of a concierge and be fed with white cheese. We wasted much time in trying to teach her the dead languages. She never could be taught to pronounce correctly the Latin for " Bonjour," as did the Pompeiian magpies. She could not say " Ave," but she said a great many other things. She was a most comical and entertaining bird, who would play at hide-and-go-seek with the children, dance the Pyrrhic dance, and fearlessly attack any number of cats, absolutely running after them and nipping the ends of their tails; which malicious act she always supplemented with a loud burst of laughter. She was as thievish as the "Gazza Ladra" herself, and equal to getting ten servants hung on false accusations. In the twinkling of an eye she would rifle every knife, fork, and spoon from the table. Money, scissors, thimbles, anything that glittered, she would seize upon and swiftly fly away with to her hiding place. As the corner where she deposited her stolen goods was well known to us all, we allowed her to do this; but the servants of a neighboring family were less indulgent, and they killed her one day because, as they stated, she had stolen a pair of new sheets, — an accusation which made us think of that minute cat in "How to succeed," which devoured four pounds of butter and only weighed three quarters of a pound after it! The master and mistress of the house scouted the idea, and turned the fools of servants off at once; but this reprisal did not mend the matter, Dame Margot's neck was none the less wrung. She was lamented by all the neighborhood, which had been kept in a state of constant diversion by her good humor and her pranks.

CHAPTER VI.

HORSES.

DO not be in a hurry to accuse us of coxcombry on seeing the heading of this chapter. Horses!—a glorious word indeed for the pen of a literary man. *Musa pedestris* (the muse goes on foot), says Horace, and all Parnassus together had but a single horse in its stable,—the well known Pegasus; and he, if we may believe Schiller's ballad, was a beast with wings, and not at all easy to harness. We are no sportsman, alas, and we deeply regret the fact, for we are as fond of horses as though we had an income of five hundred thousand francs a year, and entirely agree with the Arabs in their contempt for

people who are forced to walk. A horse
is the natural pedestal for a man, and the
perfect existence is that of the Centaur, —
that ingenious mythological invention.

However, notwithstanding that we are a
simple man of letters, we once had horses.
About the year 1843 or 1844, when engaged in sifting the sands of journalism
through the sieve of the daily newspapers,
enough golden particles appeared, to allow
of the hope that, in addition to dogs, cats,
and magpies, we might be able to find
food for a couple of pets of larger size.
At first it was a pair of Shetland ponies,
about the size of a large dog, and shaggy
as bears, who looked at us through their
long, black manes with such friendly faces
that we felt much more inclined to take
them with us into the parlor than to send
them to their stable. They helped themselves to sugar out of our pockets, just
like trained horses. For use, however,

they were entirely too small. They would have answered very well to carry an English child eight years old, or as cóach horses to Tom Thumb; but, even at that date, we were blessed with the same athletic frame as now, and crowned with the same plenteous flesh which still characterizes us, and which we have been enabled to support, without giving way under its weight, for forty consecutive years. The difference in size between master and beasts was quite too apparent to the eye, though it must be said for the ponies that they made no difficulty at all about drawing their light phaeton, to which they were fastened by a tiny harness of pale fawn-colored leather, which looked as though it might have been purchased at a toy-shop.

At that time illustrated comic journals were not so plentiful as to-day, but there were plenty in existence to caricature us and our equipage. Of course, with the exaggeration permissible in such cases, we were invested with elephantine proportions, like those of Ganesa, the Indian god of wisdom, while the ponies dwindled to the size of puppies, — or, even less, to that of rats and mice. It is true that, without great difficulty, we might have carried the little creatures, one under each arm, and the phaeton to boot upon our back. For a moment we debated the possibility of harnessing four, but this Liliputian four-in-hand would have been still more conspicuous. With great regret therefore (for we had already grown fond of the gentle creatures) we exchanged them for a pair of dappled-gray ponies of a larger size, with strong necks, wide chests, and massive shoulders, which, though far enough from being Mecklenburgers, at least looked capable of drawing grown people about. They were mares, — one named Jane and the other Betsey.

In appearance they were as much alike
as two drops of water. Never was a better
match so far as looks went; but in propor-
tion as Jane was mettlesome, Betsey was
indolent. While the former pulled at the
collar, the other trotted by her side con-
tentedly, shirking work, and giving herself
no sort of trouble. These two animals, of
the same breed, the same age, fated to live
in stalls side by side, felt for each other
the strongest antipathy. They could not
endure each other, fought in the stable,
and snapped and bit when prancing in the
traces. Nothing could reconcile them. It
was a pity too, for with their brush-like
manes cut like those of the horses of the
Parthenon, their snorting nostrils and eyes
dilated with fury, they presented rather a
triumphant appearance when going up and
down the Champs Elysées.

We were obliged to look for a substi-
tute for Betsey, and found one in a small

mare with skin of a somewhat lighter color, — for the shade we wanted could not be exactly matched. Jane approved at once of this new-comer, with whom she seemed charmed, and did the honors of the stable in the most graceful way. The tenderest friendship was soon established between them; Jane would rest her head on the shoulder of Blanche, — thus named because her shade of gray bordered on white, — and when let loose in the courtyard for an airing, they would play together like dogs or children. If one was driven out in single harness, the other, left behind, seemed sad, gave signs of feeling lonely, and, when far away she heard the hoofs of her comrade sounding on the pavement, she raised a joyful neighing like the blast of a trumpet, to which her approaching friend never failed to respond.

They came to be harnessed with remarkable docility, and would go of their own accord to their proper places on either side of the pole. Like all animals who are loved and kindly treated, Jane and Blanche soon acquired the most perfect confidence and familiarity. They would follow us about on their hind legs like dogs, and when we stood still, put their heads on our shoulders to be petted. Jane loved bread, Blanche sugar. Both of them adored watermelon rind, and there was nothing that they would not do to obtain these dainties.

If only men were not so odiously ferocious and brutal as they too often are, how happily and good-naturedly animals would play about them! This being, who can think, can speak, can do so many things which they cannot understand, fills their dimly understood thoughts, and is for them a perpetual astonishment and mystery. How frequently animals look at us with eyes which are full of questionings — questionings to which we cannot reply, as we have not the key to their language! They have a language, never-theless, by which, through sounds and in-tonations which we scarcely notice, they exchange ideas, — confused, perhaps, but still ideas, such as creatures of their sphere of sentiment and action can understand. Less stupid in this one instance than our-selves, they succeed in learning a few words of our idiom, but not enough to enable them to talk with us. These words are mostly answers to our demands upon them, so our intercourse is naturally brief. But that animals talk with each other no one can doubt who has ever lived familiarly with dogs, cats, horses, or any other sort of beasts.

As an example of this, Jane, who by nature was perfectly fearless, shying at no obstacle whatever, and afraid of noth-ing, changed her character after living

for a few months in the same stable with
Blanche, and began to exhibit sudden and
unaccountable fears. Her more timid
companion had, without doubt, told her
ghost stories at night. At times, when
dashing along in the dusk through the
Bois de Boulogne, Blanche would stop
short and shy sharply to one side as if to
avoid some phantom, which, invisible to
us, had appeared to her. Trembling all
over, with loud breathings, and body covered with sweat, she would rear straight
on end if we tried to make her go on by
touching her with the whip. Jane could
not force her to follow, however hard she
might try. In these cases there was nothing to be done but to get out, cover
Blanche's eyes and lead her along for
a few paces till the vision took flight.
Jane ended with allowing herself to be
conquered by these terrors, which Blanche,
when safely back in her stable, doubt-

less explained to her in full. We must
frankly own that when, in the middle
of a dusky lane checkered by moonlight
into fantastic lights and shadows, Blanche,
usually so docile, — Blanche, who, to ex-
cite her into a gallop, needed nothing
heavier than that whip of Queen Mab's
which was made of cricket's bone with gos-
samer lash, — planted herself suddenly on
her four feet as though some spectre had
seized her bridle, and with unconquerable
obstinacy refused to move a step forward,
we could not prevent a cold chill from
running down our spine. Searching the
shadow with unquiet glances, we almost
imagined that we could detect therein
the ghastly countenance of one of Goya's
" Caprices," where in reality were only innocent silhouettes of leafy birch-trees or
beeches.

It was one of our great pleasures to
drive these charming animals ourselves,

and an intimate understanding was soon established between us. If we held the reins in our hands, it was mainly for the look of the thing. The least click of the tongue sufficed to guide them to right or to left, to make them go slower or bring them to a stop. In a very short time they learned all our habits. They went of their own accord to the newspaper office, to the printers, to the editors, to the Bois de Boulogne, to the houses where we dined on particular days of the week, all with such exactitude that at last it became absolutely compromising. By consulting Jane or Blanche any one could have procured the address of our most mysterious visiting-places. If, while pursuing some interesting or tender conversation, we forgot the flight of time, they would recall it to our minds by neighing, and stamping with their hoofs under the balcony.

Notwithstanding the pleasantness of go-

ing about the city in a phaeton with our
little friends to pull it, we could not help
sometimes finding the wind sharp and the
rain cold, when those months came in so
fitly christened in the Republican calendar
as " Brumaire, Frimaire, Pluviôse, Ventôse,
and Nivôse." We therefore purchased a
blue coupé lined with white reps, so small
that people compared it to one belonging
to the most famous dwarf of the day, an
insult about which we were troubled very
little. A brown coupé lined with garnet
succeeded the blue, and was replaced at a
later date with one of the color of a crow's
eye upholstered with deep blue; for we
luxuriated in carriages, in spite of being
nothing but a poor scribbler, with no income stated in the big book, and no lega-
cies left us for years back; and our ponies, though nourished on literature, so to
speak, with nouns for hay, adjectives in
place of oats, and adverbs instead of straw,

were none the less fat and glossy because
of that. Alas, just then came, no one
knew exactly why, the Revolution of Feb-
ruary. Paving-stones were being dug up
on all sides to serve patriotic ends, and
the streets were no longer accessible for
wheeled vehicles. We might easily have
scaled the barricades with our agile ponies
and their light equipage, but unluckily we
had no credit left anywhere but at the
cook-shop. Horses cannot be fed on roast
chicken. The horizon was lowering with
heavy black clouds, across which red light-
nings flashed. Money took alarm, and
made haste to conceal itself. The newspaper for which we wrote suspended pub-
lication, and we thought ourselves fortu-
nate when a purchaser turned up and took
horses, harnesses, and carriages off our
hands at a quarter of their value. It was
a bitter grief to us to have them go, and
we will not swear that a salt tear or two

may not have dropped on the manes of Jane and Blanche as they were led away.

They are driven past their old home occasionally by their new owner; and always the light feet make an instant's pause under the windows, to testify that they have not forgotten the dwelling where they were once so cared for and so tenderly loved. Then we breathe a bitter and sympathetic sigh, and say in the depths of our heart, "Poor Jane! Poor Blanche! Are they happy?"

In the overwhelming of our tiny fortunes theirs is the only loss which caused us a real regret.

www.ingramcontent.com/pod-product-compliance
Lightning Source LLC
Chambersburg PA
CBHW032007010726
47493CB00007B/2304